For John Flattau:
Hero and Prince

THOMAS Y. CROWELL COMPANY   NEW YORK

The Red Lion

A TALE OF ANCIENT PERSIA

RETOLD BY DIANE WOLKSTEIN   ILLUSTRATED BY ED YOUNG

NOTES FOR THE STORYTELLER:

It is at night that the hero creeps out of his kingdom. He is running away. He seeks escape in the idyllic world of the senses, in friendship, and finally, in love. Therefore, *the roar of the lion must be shattering!* The storyteller needs to wake up both the Prince and the audience. From the moment of the roar, a new energy enters the story-consciousness, and the story unfolds with a brisk pace as the hero, in the light of day, meets his Red Lion.

D.W.

Library of Congress Cataloging in Publication Data
Wolkstein, Diane. The Red Lion. SUMMARY: Before he can be crowned King of Persia, Azgid must prove his courage by fighting the Red Lion. [1. Folklore—Iran] I. Young, Ed. II. Title. PZ8.1.W84Re 813'.5'4 [398.2] 77-3963 ISBN 0-690-01346-9 ISBN 0-690-01347-7 (lib. bdg.)

1 2 3 4 5 6 7 8 9 10

To the people of Persia

announcing:—
the sad news
of the passing
of our great,
venerable king

Vatmekollim

he will be succeeded by his
honorable son the brave
Azgid who, after a period
of mourning, will engage
in mortal combat with
our fierce lion as in our
ancient tradition

of Persia

When the King of Persia died, there was great weeping, for he had been a brave and wise leader. Yet in little more than a month the mourning would be over, and the King's son, Azgid, would be crowned. But before the Prince could be crowned he would have to prove his courage just as every Prince before him had done, by fighting the Red Lion.

One day during this time the Vizier went to the young Prince and urged him to prepare himself for the contest. Azgid trembled. He had always been afraid of lions. And the Red Lion was the most ferocious of lions. He decided to run away.

That night, when it was very dark, he crept out of his bedroom, mounted his horse, and rode off.

He rode two days
and nights. On the
morning of the third
day he entered a
grove of trees and
heard a sweet melo-
dy. Dismounting, he
walked quietly until
he saw a shepherd,
sitting in a clearing
and playing a flute.
All about him his
sheep stood listening.

"God be with you," said the shepherd to the stranger.

"And with you," the Prince replied, "but please do not stop your song."

The shepherd took up his flute and played for the clouds, for the winds, for his sheep, and for the stranger.

When he finished, Azgid spoke: "Surely you are wondering who I am. I wish I could tell you my name. But it is a secret that must stay locked in my heart. I beg you to believe me, I am no enemy. I am an honorable youth who has been forced to flee from his home."

"You are welcome to stay with me," the shepherd answered. "I would be glad of your company and I can show you a place that will cause you to forget your troubles."

Hour after hour the Prince and the shepherd walked, the Prince leading his horse and the sheep following behind the shepherd. As the sun was setting they came to the most beautiful valley Azgid had ever seen. It was perfectly quiet and Azgid and the shepherd sat and gazed in wonder at the hills in front of

them. Then suddenly the shepherd jumped up.

"Time to go!" he said.

"But why must we leave so quickly?" asked the Prince. "Can there be any place on earth more lovely?"

"It *is* beautiful," the shepherd agreed. But then he raised his sleeve, revealing a long, cruel, red scar. He traced his finger along the scar and said: "Lions! Once I was late returning to the village and the village gates were closed. This is the result. I do not want it to happen a second time."

"Then return to the village with the sheep," the Prince said, "but I cannot stay with you." He mounted his horse and rode north.

He rode two days and nights, and on the third morning he came to a desert. He and his horse were tired and hungry and thirsty. The wind blew sand in his face and he was riding with his eyes half-shut when suddenly his horse neighed. Through the streaming sands Azgid saw the tents of an Arab camp. His horse began to prance but he pulled back on the bridle and continued to ride slowly to show that his was a peaceful visit.

An Arab Sheik greeted him with courtesy. He offered the Prince food and had his horse fed and cared for.

After the Prince had eaten he said to the Sheik: "Forgive me if I do not reveal my name. Because of certain troubles it is a secret that must stay locked in my heart. But I have jewels and precious stones I would gladly give you if you would allow me to remain with you."

"You are our guest," the Sheik replied, and he refused to accept any of the Prince's treasures.

The following morning the Sheik provided the Prince with a magnificent stallion, and for the next three days the Prince rode with the Sheik and his companions hunting antelope.

On the third evening the Sheik spoke to the Prince: "My men are pleased with your spirit," he said, "and with your skill at hunting. But soon there will be a battle. My men want to know if they can rely on your strength and courage. To the south lies a range of hills known as the Red Hills. It is lion country. Ride there tomorrow on the stallion. Take your sword and spear, and bring us back the hide of one of these fierce lions to show us we can count on you on the day of battle."

That night, when it was very still, the Prince slipped out of his tent. He stroked the beloved stallion he had ridden and whispered good-bye in his ear. Then he mounted his own horse and rode west.

After two days and nights he came to a country of rolling meadows and green fields. There in the distance was a splendid red sandstone palace.

At the gates the Prince took off his ring and asked the guard to present it to the Emir. Immediately he was invited to enter the palace.

As the Prince was explaining his situation to the Emir, Perizide, the Emir's daughter, appeared. The Emir, who was impressed with Azgid's good manners and fine speech, said to his daughter, "My child, show this young man our palace and gardens, and be certain he is invited to the entertainment this evening."

Perizide led the Prince through room after room and then out into the garden. There were flowers and trees of every kind in the garden and in the middle was an oval-shaped pool filled with rose water. In the water floated one perfect lily. It was perfect and yet not as beautiful as Perizide.

After dinner in the cool evening air, Perizide herself provided the entertainment. She played the lute and sang. As Azgid listened, he felt his soul rising higher and higher. "That is why I have run away," he thought, "so I might find Perizide."

"RRRAAGGGGGH!"

"What was *that?*" cried the Prince, jumping to his feet.

"Oh, that's just our guard Boulak. He's yawning."

"*Yawning?*" repeated the Prince.

"Yes," said Perizide. "He does that when it is late. I will say good night now."

After Perizide left, the Emir stood up. "It is late for me, too. Come, I will show you to your bedroom."

They had just begun to climb the staircase when Azgid looked up. His hand froze on the banister. There at the top of the landing was an enormous lion.

"Oh, that's just Boulak," said the Emir. "He's perfectly harmless. He never attacks unless someone is afraid of him."

"Oh I'm not, ah, quite r-r-ready for, ah, I'm not r-ready for s-s-sleep," faltered the Prince.

"Well then, come up when you wish," said the Emir. "Yours is the first bedroom on the right."

Azgid backed down the stairs. He backed down the corridor and into the music room and locked the doors. He sat on a chair and waited. Soon he heard the lion padding down the stairs. He heard him claw at the door. The door shook. The lion roared.

"RRAAAGGGH!" Azgid thought the lion would tear down the door and devour him, but he just sat there. He did not try to run away. He waited. The lion roared again. "RRAAAAAAGGH!"

Azgid listened. The lion roared a third time. Suddenly Azgid realized the roars were not threats. They were warnings. They were telling him: Three times you have run away. If you run away again—wherever you may go—a lion will be waiting.

A lion would always be waiting for him until he went home to fight his own lion.

Azgid listened. Boulak did not roar again. Then he heard the lion padding up the stairs.

Early the next morning, Azgid explained that he had to return home at once. He mounted his horse and, thinking only of the Red Lion, rode day and night until he reached the palace.

At the appointed time Azgid entered the crowded arena. The Emir, Perizide, the Sheik, and the shepherd were all there, seated in the stands. But Azgid did not look up. No, his eyes were on the doors from which the Red Lion would emerge. He waited.

The doors opened.
The lion sprang out.
Azgid stood firm, his
spear in his hand.
The lion roared and
leapt—

—right over the head of Azgid. When Azgid whirled around to throw his spear, he saw the Red Lion lying on his back, playfully waving his paws in the air like a happy puppy. Then the lion trotted up to Azgid and affectionately licked his hands.

The Red Lion was tame. Every lion who had ever fought a Prince of Persia had been tame. Only fear would make him ferocious.

And so Azgid was crowned King of Persia. And in due time he married Perizide, and the two lived together happily and ruled their kingdom wisely and well.